Gypsy Lore

*The Culture, Life and History of the
Travelling Gypsies in Europe;
the Stories of the Romani People*

By Robert Andrew Scott Macfie

Published by Pantianos Classics

ISBN-13: 978-1986303750

First published in 1908

Contents

About the Author... *iv*
Introduction..*viii*
Gypsy Lore 10
Notes... 48

About the Author

Robert Andrew Scott Macfie (1868 - 1935) was an author and academic, born to a prominent family of sugar manufacturers in Liverpool who were bought out by the Tate and Lyle company. As a young man he volunteered for service in the British Army, gaining perspective on the military and its organization in the process.

Possessed of a keen intellect, Macfie researched and wrote many essays and books regarding gypsy folklore – a field in which he became a respected authority. Compiling and organizing many stories of Romani peoples, he would stage meetings with different traveller communities who visited the UK from Continental Europe in a bid to gain knowledge on their way of life and stories of yore.

In 1913 Macfie accompanied a group of Gypsy horse traders to Bulgaria – an adventure in which observed much of a culture little-known in Western Europe. These escapades were recorded in a book entitled "With Gypsies in Bulgaria". Such scholarly activities were disrupted by the outbreak of World War I – although in his mid-forties at the time, Macfie's education and experience were viewed as ideal for an officer, and he signed up for the war effort.

The prolific writing for which he was held in high regard continued throughout the war. As with many soldiers, initial enthusiasm gave way to disillusion and finally disgust with how the costly and hopelessly administered conflict cost so many lives. Robert Macfie sent the following letter to his brother in 1916:

"The want of preparation, the vague orders, the ignorance of the objective & geography, the absurd

haste, and in general the horrid bungling were scandalous. After two years of war it seems that our higher commanders are still without common sense. In any well-regulated organisation a divisional commander would be shot for incompetence- here another regiment is ordered to attempt the same task in the same muddling way. It was worse than Hooge, much worse - and it is still going on!"

Macfie was one of the few of his company to survive the entirety of the war; complaining of loneliness, the veteran said he did not like the fresh-faced conscripts who arrived to replace his experienced and mature fallen comrades. Noted by other author's as a man of great spirit, Macfie was skilled at raising funds which were used to pay for luxuries such as cocoa and whist tournaments; things which kept some morale in the Liverpool Scottish regiment in which he served. In the later part of the war he organized a beer garden in a village pasture, in which soldiers were urged to 'bring their own pots' to receive ale and other refreshments.

Returning from the war a changed man, Macfie published a cookbook; the hard conditions of the front made cooking decent meals as much about invention as availability. In 1920, he published a retrospective memoir of his time in the war, entitled A Mother of France. The remaining fifteen years of his life were spent quietly, with occasional contributions to the Gypsy Lore Society.

Introduction

The following work was produced in the early 20th century by the leading reviver of the Gypsy Lore Society. Dormant for over fifteen years, it was on the suggestion of friends that the author, in 1907, obtained a headquarters for the society in Liverpool, United Kingdom. He and other members began to publicize research and works concerning Romani folklore. Copies of this work and others were distributed to academic authorities.

Between a series of cultural allusions and details, the author sets out the mission of the society; to assemble, examine and discuss the folklore, myths and legends of the Gypsy Traveller peoples. He includes insightful commentary of the traditions and behavior of these groups around Europe, noting both their reputation and their achievements. We learn how gypsies are renowned for their abilities in musicmaking and dance, and how their storytelling is rich in tradition; authors over centuries, fascinated by the Romani peoples, recorded some of their finer tales.

Today, the Gypsy Lore Society is headquartered in the United States. It publishes various newsletters and stages regular meetings around the USA and Europe. Its core mission – of finding and discussing gypsy folklore – remains unchanged. Scholarly papers and contributions are encouraged, and the Society maintains strong ties with universities around the world.

Gypsy Lore

Under the late Pope's rule it is said that festivals at the Vatican were characterized by an abundance of gold plate and a scarcity of victuals. In Gypsy literature what is most conspicuous is the number of books and the small amount of knowledge. Mr. George F. Black's Bibliography, of which the Gypsy Lore Society is about to publish a preliminary issue, contains nearly two thousand titles; yet Gypsy lore bristles with as many unsolved problems as the Gypsy hedgehog, whose Anglo-Romani name is itself a mystery, has spines.

Nor is this the result, or lack of result, due to any neglect of the subject by the greater scholars, as some imagine who suppose that the literary wanderings of the nomad Gypsy are circumscribed by the boundaries of the Belles Lettres..."Not the great Pott?" exclaimed the librarian of an ancient university, when I mentioned the author of *Die Zigeuner in Europa und Asien*, shocked that so eminent a philologist could have given attention to so mean a people...Granted that, in libretti, plays and fiction, the picturesque Romanichel occupies more than his share of the boards, a large section of the books devoted to his race might, on the other hand, be described as "revoltingly learned."

It was at least three hundred and sixty years ago that merry Andrew Borde, drinking in a tavern, to judge from the topics of his conversation, met a Gypsy band and recorded thirteen phrases of what he believed to be "Egipt Speche." He was followed by Joseph Scaliger, who, in 1597, contributed to a rare little volume by Vulcanius, *De Literis et Lingtca Getarum*, a vocabulary of seventy-one words and the important generalisation that the Gypsies spoke, not an artificial jargon like Rotwelsh or Shelta, but a true language,— *propriam sibi ac peculiarem provinciae e qua orti fuerunt linguam habuisse*. And to his judgment and authority his editor readily assented:—not so the "man in the street," who to this day believes that Romani is "gibberish," and would be frankly incredulous if told that its noun possesses nine cases. Scaliger seems to have had no disciples, for during the two succeeding centuries only four additions were made to the Gypsy vocabulary:— Ludolfus, 1691; the *Waldheimer Lexikon*, 1726; De la Croze, 1741; and the *Beytrag but Rotwellischen Grammatik*, 1755 : but the discovery by Rudiger, about 1777, that Romani is related to the tongues of India aroused interest and stimulated research, so that when, in 1844-5 Pott undertook the herculean task of proving that all European dialects have a common origin, he was able to enumerate no less than fifty Quellen.

Pott's work was crowned by the French Academy, and the language of the despised Gypsy, weirdly attractive and most difficult of culture, became the orchid of the philological garden. Romani, good, bad and indifferent, was collected greedily; the making of many books went on apace; and Pott's labours were continued brilliantly by the great scholars Ascoli and Miklosich, now, alas! no more, and by Finck, Kuhn, Pischel and Wackemagel. But the outstanding event of this fruitful period was the publication by Paspati of a dialect which he justly described as "la langue-mere de tous les Tchinghianes eparpilles en Europe, et en Amerique." It is with difficulty that I refrain from quoting, from the sad and poetic introductions to the book which he printed in 1870, long passages depicting the devotion with which this ideal Romany Rai applied himself to his task. Suffice it to say that the noble physician endured with unfailing patience every kind of unpleasantness, and conquered inconceivable difficulties, in order to secure the standard of pure Romani from the nomad Gypsies of Rumelia, "grand type du vrai Tchinghiane" ... "dont la misere, Tavilis-sement et la brutalité, ne se rencontrent dans aucune race nomadique connue," and from their sedentary brethren at Constantinople " aussi pauvres et aussi miserables que leurs freres les Nomades, et infiniment plus adonnés qu'eux, au vol et a la ruse."

    Disappointing are the results of all this labour. The Aryan basis of the language, the fact of its connection with the tongues of India, and the unity of origin of all the European varieties are established: and the loan-words have been isolated and classified. But to the simple question " What was the origin [1] of the Gypsies?" garrulous philology can still return no straightforward reply.

Pischel points a hesitating finger to the Hindu Kush: Grierson hints that Gypsy is not Indian at all, but one of the Pisaca languages, a group which, he believes, " left the parent stem after the Indo-Aryan languages, but before all the typical Iranian characteristics, which we meet in the Avesta, had become developed." More knowledge is required; ampler collections of every dialect, and in particular a thorough study of the Gypsies of Asia of whom almost nothing is known. Are there in our Universities no enthusiasts ready to sacrifice worldly success in the hope of adding their page to the history of a people more mysterious and more ubiquitous than the Jews, by following old Glanvill's scholar-Gypsy—

"Of pregnant parts and quick inventive brain,

Who, tired of knocking at preferment's door,
One summer-morn forsook
His friends, and went to learn the gipsy-lore,
And roam'd the world with that wild brotherhood.
And came, as most men deem'd, to little good."

And for those, less ambitious, who prefer the seclusion of the study to the bustle of the tents, there are many little philological conundrums which may pleasantly engage attention besides the great " Gypsy Riddle.' Entertainment may be found in the dissection of words and phrases written down by collectors who had no Romani:—the *shuckerakerbenhikoles*, "eloquent," of the Beytrag of 1755; *gegernachew leha*, "gimlet," in the Sulzer Zigeunerliste of 1787, or Jacob Bryant's *water jam perall*, "to fly." Moreover the search for vocabularies, manuscript and printed, which have not yet been analysed and added to the Gypsy *copia verborum* is not exhausted. Walter Whiter, the unsound but round philologist of Borrow's *Lavengro,* who believed that languages are derived from the earth, boasted in the preface to his *Etymologicon Magnum*, 1800, " in our own age a language has been lost: it shall be my province to record and preserve another." And he did indeed collect from a " venerable Braminess " the deepest and best specimens of English Romani which are known; but, with the exception of a few words which he incorporated in his etymological books, they would all have perished had not Lady Arthur Grosvenor, in August this year, most fortunately discovered a copy of extracts from his lost *Lingua Cingariana*.

Whence springs the attractiveness of Romani? Partly perhaps from its very difficulty, for it has become the gymnasium of linguistic exercises: or contrariwise, if we may neglect as exceptional the case of Pott, who confessed to Groome that once only in his life had he spoken with living Gypsies, from the facility of studying an oriental language in Europe from the human document. But if it be the part of a fool to cast pearls before swine, it is as surely the duty of the sage to rescue the jewels from its sty. And it may be that in the contrast between the glittering gems and the obscurity of the source from which they are recovered lies much of the fascination of Gypsy research. Not even the philologist can expel with a pitchfork the romantic element of his nature, and Romani is the one philological romance. It is no mere medium for the exchange of elementary thought—rather is it the vellum, tattered and crumpled from much use, stained and decayed by long exposure, on which in faded characters that cannot yet be clearly read, is recorded the history of a race. Or shall we compare it with a *breccia* marble in which if the clay matrix reveal an Indian origin, each individual loan-word, like each individual pebble, may add its contribution to our knowledge of Gypsy migrations. Thus *trushul* indicates an ancient familiarity with the blood-stained trident of the great god Shiva, and *doriav, tschikat, drom, lovina,* halts in countries where Persian, Armenian, Greek and old Slavonic were spoken. Moreover, Romani has the antique beauty of a crumbling ruin, and presents the profoundly interesting spectacle of a language in various stages of decay, succumbing gradually to different diseases, here overwhelmed by the infiltration of alien words, there losing its own inflections and adopting the grammatical costume of its British or Spanish hosts.

From the linguistic side only one view of the Gypsies is obtained, and that not the most interesting. It has been more studied than the others, and is given precedence here because Romani is the passport to the confidence of these wild children of nature. They take an inordinate pride in their tongue,—" nous parlons comme les oiseaux chantent, nous chantons comme les lions rugissent" was their brag to Vaillant,—and he who imagines he can penetrate behind the mask they wear, without a knowledge of their language, imagines a vain thing.

Records and historical traditions the Gypsies have none. On the stage of European history they were cast for a "thinking part." Nor did they generally court publicity, as Samuel Rowlands testified in *The Runnagates Race or the Originall of Regiment of Rogues*, being part of *Martin Mark-all*, published in
1610: "these kinde of people lived more quietly and out of harme in respect of the other sort, making themselves as strangers, and would never put forth themselves in any tumult or Commotion, as the other sort [the ' canting caterpillars' under Cocke Lorrell did; but what vice they exercised not one way, they were not inferior to them in the like, or rather worse another way." The chroniclers

noticed them only when they became an intolerable nuisance; at other times they were neglected as beneath contempt. They first attracted the attention of Western Europe in 1417 (the very year in -which Alexander the Good had granted the Gypsies of Moldavia " the air and earth to wander, and fire and iron to forge"), by abandoning their ordinary avocation of smiths and invading the Hanseatic towns as pilgrims from Little Egypt. [2] Their choice of disguise, and the legend they offered as an explanation of their pilgrimage, showed great ingenuity and an intimate acquaintance with the customs and superstitions of the time and place. As pilgrims they could live the vagrant life they loved, avoid the labour they hated; and claim the advantages of gentle or even noble birth, albeit they were, as Dekker described them, "beggerly in apparell, barbarous in condition, beastly in behauior; and bloudy if they meet aduantage."

Of the legend with which the Gypsies hocussed, not only the Emperor Sigismund, but also the Pope of Rome, there are several versions. I quote that given by C. B. L. M. V. R., the author of *Zwey nutzliche Tractdtlein Das Erste: Wunderliche und wahrhaffttge Beschreibung der Cingaren oder Ziegeuner*, 1664, which connects the Gypsies with the Magi, a tradition not unimportant in explaining the introduction of the Morris dance into England, and, possibly, the dissemination of carols:—

"They had been Christians at the first: or rather, as some pretend, their earliest Christian ruler was the Moorish King, who, according to the opinion of Papists, was called Caspar, and was one of the three Magi who came to Bethlehem at the time of Christ's birth, to offer and present gold, frankincense and myrrh to the new-born King of the Jews, that is to say, the dear Christ-child. Through him they were originally converted to the Christian faith, but yet not quite confirmed therein until after Christ's ascension, when the apostles and disciples of the Lord were sent out into all the world, and some coming to them, fully established them in the Christian doctrine. But when afterwards, under the heathen emperors, persecutions endured for long, they allowed themselves to be perverted and fell again from the Christian religion into paganism. Nevertheless they soon repented their apostasy. Wherefore seven years afterwards they turned again to Christ, and their fellow-Christians, who had remained faithful, laid on them the penance for their sin that they must wander hither and thither, in affliction and exile, as vagrants for seven years, after the expiry of which time they were to return home."

How they performed their penance, scouring Europe in disorderly gangs, dividing, re-uniting, and in general behaving exactly as our so-called " German" Gypsy visitors behaved in 1906, and how they did not return to Egypt, nor to any other home, when the seven years had expired, has been described by Bataillard who collected an extraordinary number of early references to the invasion, far out-distanced his predecessors Thomasius (1671), Grellmann (1787), and Heister

(1842), and made this interesting corner of history his own. Yet his theory of Gypsy origin has not been accepted, and, excellent as is his work on the immigration and dispersion of the Gypsies in Western Europe, it would be a mistake to assume that nothing will ever be added to it. Gypsy history, modern as well as ancient, is necessarily based upon fragmentary side-lights from legal records, proclamations, town accounts and the like, and on documents, often unpublished, which deal principally with other subjects. It can only be written piecemeal, by many workers each investigating a country or district, and though a considerable number of such monographs have been printed, much remains to be done. Not all can follow the example of Thesleff, who, to obtain material for his account oi the Gypsies in Finland, employed four persons to search the local newspapers of 1771 to 1897, an eight years' task; but there are few who cannot advance historical study by seeking out and sending to the *Journal of the Gypsy Lore Society* references from books, tracts or ephemeral literature, or, better still, from parish registers and other manuscripts,—facts isolated perhaps, but precious as the fragments of the Portland vase, and destined ultimately to be pieced together to form a comprehensive history of the Gypsy race.

And if during comparatively recent times the Romane have been enveloped in a twilight of mysterious doubt, their history before 1417 is, and seems likely to remain, in Cimmerian darkness. Not that there is any lack of speculations; but few of them are even plausible. With admirable consistency the Gypsies everywhere declared themselves Egyptians, and Thomasius, whose erudition is more remarkable than his insight into the character of the people about whom he was writing, indignantly reproved those who doubted their word,— *"Wenn sie nun in Anfange so fromm und ehrlich sich erzeiget, so solte man ihnen dock wohl einigen Glauben beymessen."* Even in the nineteenth century the good Samuel Roberts supported their claim, but apparently only because he could find nobody else to fulfil the prophesies of Isaiah. They have been identified with the descendants of Cain, the Sigynnae of Herodotus, refugees from the Cities of the Plain, priests of Isis, Tartars, Chaldeans,

Sudras, German Jews, and Druids. Before discussing half-a-dozen views which "s'approchferent d'une plus probable apparence de vérité" the Marquis Colocci cites some fifty extravagant guesses, of which a score at least are built upon the sand of a similarity of designation. The unconscious *Zigeuner* has been served heir to every nation, historical or mythological, which happened to have a *z* or a *g* in its name, or to any race whose habits seemed similar in any respect. One theory is worth mentioning which derives the word Cingarus from the κίγκλος of Menander's verse, πτωχότερος ει λεβηρίδος και κιγκάλου because although the etymology, which was invented by Johannes Baptista Pius and supported by an array of scholars including Erasmus, is false, it may throw light on the interesting superstition from which the Gypsy Lore Society derives its badge and motto. The κίγκλος was the water-wagtail, ancient type of beggary, which was said to have no nest of its own, and to which the epithet "much-wandering" was applied, idianus records that the name *Cincli* was used proverbially by peasants to mean tramps, and Thomasius quotes the merry poet Euridicus Cordus who employed it to describe his own poverty;—

> *Sat jam sat miser hinc et inde Cinclus*
> *Erravi: propriam semel domunculam*
> *Felix cochlea possidere vellem.*

"May not Gypsies have been led," asks Groome, "by the resemblance of its name to theirs, to adopt the water-wagtail as the Gypsy bird ?" Certain it is that in Germany, as in Great Britain, it is the *Romano tschiriklo*, and that its appearance foretells a meeting with Gypsies. The one theory which, based on ample historical evidence, gives a date and a reason for the Gypsy exodus from India, is that of de Goeje, the eminent Professor of Arabic at Leyden. He shows that the Indian name *Jat* was first introduced into Western Asia by the twelve thousand minstrels imported towards the end of his reign (a.d. 420—438) by the Persian King Bahram Djour. Among Persian and Arab authors the word, with its Arab pronunciation *Zott,* became in process of time a generic term for any people originating from the valley of the Indus, and was in this sense applied to the tribes, probably of mixed races, which driven by famine as Masudi relates in his *Tanbih,* entered Persia and formed the great emigration of the beginning of the ninth century. Among these invaders de Goeje places the Gypsies (Zott, Nawar, etc) of Western Asia, and he further seeks successfully to connect them with the European Gypsies by a comparison of their dialects. This theory is so well founded historically that it can only be controverted on historical grounds. It would therefore seem to be the duty of philologists to revise their hypotheses in its light, by admitting that, in the emigration of the ninth century, tribes may have been present who spoke languages which were the origin of modem Romani.

Gypsy study is in the unfortunate position of a ship with two chronometers which indicate different times. A third method of determining the origin of the race is much to be desired, in order that its indication may decide whether philology or history points to the truth. If it be a fact that four eminent anthropologists examined the pygmies last year, and each obtained a different result, the layman may well doubt the reliability of their methods: yet these same savants complain that philologists submit linguistic evidence to a strain greater than it can bear. Here then is a challenge:—I propose, as touchstone for the science of physical anthropology, the problem of Gypsy origin. The material can be found, in great abundance and considerable purity, near home. Let the man with the tape and rule measure a few thousand Gypsies, and then declare precisely with what Asiatic race they are most closely allied. And in his researches may not the geographer assist by pointing out what routes were possible at the time of the Gypsy migration? Incidentally he will find much else to interest him. The results of close-breeding can be studied in Wales, where he may meet robust Gypsies in whose pedigrees almost every union for five successive generations has been between first cousins. In Servia and the Bukowina he may investigate the little-known "white Gypsies." And everywhere he will admire the racial assertiveness which causes the descendants of mixed marriages to revert to the Gypsy rather than to the *Gajo* type.

This racial assertiveness, this amazingly strong nationality, this innate tenacity for everything that is Gypsy, is the greatest miracle of a race which lives and moves in an atmosphere of wonders. With other folk needless languages tend to decay. The patriotic Irish and the clannish Scots rapidly lose their Gaelic abroad. Unwritten tongues elsewhere split into innumerable dialects. Australia boasts at least two hundred; Crawford counted forty in Timor for a hundred-thousand inhabitants; and in New Guinea Erdweg found four for 294 persons. Yet the Gypsies of Wales and Turkey speak to-day practically the same language although it is five centuries since diey separated. One other race has preserved its nationality, although scattered in apparently isolated groups throughout the civilised world, living like a parasite within an organism of which it forms no part: but it is bound together by the bonds of an ancient religion. The Gypsies have neither religion nor religious sense. [3] " In the world," say the Servian *Cigani,* "there are seventy-seven and a half religions: the half is the Gypsies'." They cheerfully adopt whatever form of worship. Christian or Mahommedan, is most profitable at the moment, and change as often as may be convenient. In comparison with them, the Vicar of Bray was a bigot. At the beginning of the last century British missionary enthusiasm resolved to test itself with the reagent nearest to hand: "the success," as one of the leaders reported, was, "next to an entire failure;" the disappointed missionaries went further afield where either the results were more encouraging or the failures less conspicuous; and the heathen Gypsies were left to go their own godless ways. They are the despair of the philanthropist, who, because he lives in a villa, thinks that nomads should be packed in slums. Countless decrees of banishment, repressive measures, attempts at compulsory civilisation, and even friendly offers of affluence and comfort as we conceive it, have left the Gypsies exactly where they were. The extraordinary differences in manner of thought, ambitions, and life, which separate them from the people among whom they live, are maintained as sharply as ever. The late Archduke Josef of Austria, a prince deeply versed in Gypsy lore and author of a Romani grammar and dictionary, squandered a fortune in his attempt to persuade his proteges to settle. He might as well have built rabbit-hutches and invited the conies to leave their burrows. For the *Wan-*

derlust is more deeply rooted in the Gypsy than in the Bedouin, — "il préfére mourir sous sa tente, que de se sentir opprime par les murailles et le plafond des chambres."

With their instinct for wandering the Gypsies inherit certain professions. Everywhere they are known as entertainers, kettle-menders, small smiths, horse-dealers, or makers of sieves, baskets, and clothes pegs. There is nothing remarkable in the fact that they follow these callings. They are those by which nomads, the world over, are obliged by their manner of life to earn their support; and in places where, or at times when, methods of rapid transit are undeveloped there is a need for vagrants who ply such trades. What is remarkable is the eminence which Gypsies have attained in them. "They do few things," said Arthur Symons, "but they do these things better than others... They dance in Spain, they play in Hungary: they are better dancers than the Spaniards in their national dances, and they play Hungarian music better than the Hungarians."

Whether Gypsy music, with its special scale and intervals less than a semitone, is oriental or not is a problem of only academic interest. But whether the music of the Hungarian Gypsies is Gypsy or Hungarian is a fiercely disputed question. Patriotic Hungarians contend that the Gypsies filched their ancient dances and airs, to mutilate them beyond recognition. Would that they had done the same for British melody! And at one time this result, which might have preserved many a folksong now lost, must have seemed possible; for until recently the country districts of England were dependent on Gypsies for entertainment as exclusively as is the western Orient to-day. In the beginning of the eighteenth century they entered Wales playing violins, but seized the triple harp and for a time drove the native musicians out of the profession. In highland regiments the wild genius of Caird pipers distinguishes them from their Scots comrades. Nowadays a rural police on bicycles, and the enclosure of the common lands, have driven the Gypsies to the suburbs of great towns where music halls rob them of the appreciative audience which alone made it possible to create in Hungary a national art. For the Gypsies were for centuries the sole exponents of Hungarian music, the existence of which was unknown until they made it popular, and the argument of the Hungarian patriots is as weak as would be the contention that Beethoven's thirty-three variations on a waltz by Diabelli were by Diabelli himself. On unrecorded fleeting Gypsy improvisations Listz founded his rhapsodies, but future generations will know as little of Gypsy as is now known of Greek music from the Delphic ode, if they must depend on these translations into the musical language of civilized Europe.

If the Gypsies took and transformed the music of the Hungarians, just as it is said they can take and transform a horse, so that the original owners cannot recognise it, they have on the other hand brought with them presents from the East. There is a tradition, supported by some internal evidence, that it was they who introduced playing cards into Europe. Chiromancy will be granted ungrudgingly, and also the form of confidence trick which Borrow described under the name of *Hokkano Baro*, as efficacious to-day on the banks of the Brahmaputra as it is, with slight modifications, in our own enlightened land. Europe's gratitude for these endowments is perhaps not greater than the gratitude of the Trojans to the Greeks; but there is one gift, a delight from childhood to old age, which should win for the Romanichels a warm place in our affections, if, as Groome brought much evidence to prove, it is to them we owe it,—the gift of fairy tales. That most of the popular stories of Europe are traceable to Indian originals is admitted. Who but the Gypsies, exercising their talents as professional story-tellers and adding to their original stock, while they wandered from the East and spread themselves throughout the civilised West, could have been the channel through which these stories were disseminated? The proof lies in the collection of Gypsy folk-tales in every district, and their comparison with variants obtained from Gypsy and *Gajo* sources elsewhere. When Groome wrote, in 1899, only 160 Gypsy folk-tales were known, but the number is gradually increasing and each new find adds its little to the weight of his argument. What more delightful occupation could be imagined than this search, and what reward more ample than the triumph with which Sampson, last summer in the mountains of Wales, recorded from Gypsy lips a story which is also to be found in the *Arabian Nights*.

The Gypsies are a mine, not only of folk-tales, but also of much kindred folk-lore,—songs, customs, superstitions,—for .the recovery of which few save Liebich and Wlislocki have laboured systematically. Yet Gypsy customs have great ethnological importance. One extraordinary, almost incredible, example is die fact that in this twentieth century, and here in Great Britain, funeral sacrifices are comparatively common. What is the explanation.? Not fear of infection as has been suggested, for the Gypsy knows how easy it is to disinfect jewellery: yet Kenza Boswell threw into the Mersey all his father Westerns property, including gold watches and chains, which could not be consumed by fire. Not, we may be sure, to avoid bickering among the relations, which is the excuse generally given: for when his wife died, only last year, old Isaac Heron reduced himself to poverty by burning his own van and everything in it. Rather must it be some subconscious belief that the treasured possessions of the dead are thus sent to follow them into the next world. Who, capable of sympathising even with the follies of others, will win the confidence of our veteran Gypsies and discover this and other secrets before they are lost for ever?

 It would be easy to multiply such instances, for Gypsy Lore is a gem of many facets, scintillating with interests of every hue. In its study each will find something of special interest. Even for the toxicologist there is the method, just discovered independently by two Romany Rais, by which the Romane were wont to *drab balos*. But the race is already bending to the pressure of modern civilisation, and as, one by one, the older Gypsies are placed in their graves, priceless knowledge is buried with them, —a funeral sacrifice which science cannot regard with indifference. The harvest is more than ripe; it is rotting in the fields: and if reapers be not forthcoming it will be lost irretrievably. That is why the Gypsy Lore Society [4] appeals to those who are qualified by a university education to observe exactly and record correctly, to apply themselves to the study of Gypsies while there are yet Gypsies left to study.

R. A. Scott Macfie.

Notes

[1] Linguistic origin must generally be understood, for a race of nomads may never have had any geographical origin.
[2] Not necessarily from the banks of the Nile, but possibly from districts named "Little Egypt" in Epirus or Asia Minor.
[3] Yet why should a race which has no religion make pilgrimages to the shrine of Saint Sara at Saintes-Maries-de-la-Mer? And is there any truth in the theory that it is not Saint Sara, but an altar of Mithra in her crypt, which is the object of veneration. Who knows! Who will investigate?
[4] The address is: Gypsy Lore Society, 6 Hope Place, Liverpool, Great Britain.

Made in the USA
Middletown, DE
27 March 2021